FRANKLIN PARK PUBLIC LIBRARY
3 1316 00412 9154

To Nooni, who taught me the most important things of all.

Orit Gidali

Nora the Mind Reader

www.enchantedlionbooks.com

First American Edition published in 2012 by
Enchanted Lion Books, 20 Jay Street, Studio M-18, Brooklyn, NY 11201
Published by arrangement with Kinneret Zmora-Bitan Publishing, Or Yehuda, Israel

ISBN 978-1-59270-120-9
Printed in May 2012 in China by South China printing Co. Ltd.

Orit Gidali

Nora the Mind Reader

Illustrations by Aya Gordon-Noy

Translated from the Hebrew by Annette Appel

ENCHANTED LION BOOKS
NEW YORK

When Nora came home from Kindergarten one day,
she told her mommy how a boy in her class had said to her:

And even though she didn't know exactly what a flamingo was,
she was insulted. Very insulted.

So her mom sat her down and gave her a great big hug.

Then she went to look for something important.
Very important.

Now where is that magic wand?

She looked high and low
before she found it –
her special wand for days
that don't seem to be filled
with any magic at all.

When Nora picked up the magic wand, something incredible happened. Suddenly she could see what people were saying as well as what they were really thinking.

My legs are tired.
I REALLY want some chocolate!
This is so boring!
CHOCOLATE! NOW!
And drinking is good for you, right?
I want a can of soda, too!
Want a bite?
Not a bit.
Yuck! Yick!
You have nice legs.
Such yummy drumsticks!

Peering through her wand, Nora saw that people don't always say what they think, or say what they think they are saying.

I get it!
I think I get it...

The next day, Nora carried her magic wand all the way to school. As soon as she got there, she looked through it at the boy who had hurt her feelings.

After that, Nora tried looking through her magic wand at other children, especially when they said things that weren't very nice.

With the help of her magic wand, Nora saw something strange happen whenever kids said mean things.

She saw that words that often started out as nice turned into hurtful ones as they flew from people's thoughts into their mouths.

So getting insulted didn't really make sense.

But moping around and not doing anything didn't make sense either.
Blu
Blu
I'd
love to
get out of
this bowl!

Nora thought and thought, until she finally knew what to do.

She went up to the boy who had hurt her feelings and told him just what she thought of him.

"You have a nice smile," she said, and she meant it.
Then she invited him over to her house to play.

And Harry (for that was his name) said,
"I'll come!"

Do you have firecrackers at your house?

I have fireworks going off in my tummy.

I feel so funny.

“Hooray!” cried Nora. “You have to promise, though, that you won’t call me names ever again.”

But there was no need to worry, because in a split second, “flamingo legs” flew out of Harry’s head, and he gave Nora the great big smile she really liked.

At the end of the day, Nora gave the magic wand back to her mom and told her everything that had happened at school that day.

Now I know how to make magic without a wand!

Nora's mom gave her a great big hug. She was happy because her little girl always reminded her of the most important things of all.

Now Nora's mom didn't need the magic wand any more either, so she left it in the yard to be found by someone else.

Then…

A neighbor's dog found the wand.

Bow!
Wow!
Wow!
Wow!

From then on, he started barking less
and wagging his tail more.

And all his days were filled with magic.

Mommy, now let ME read you the story.
I'll do anything not to go to sleep yet.
Nora the Mind Reader